Bittersweet

Aliya DalRae

Bittersweet Copyright © 2017 by Aliya DalRae
All rights reserved.

First Edition, 2017

This is a work of fiction. All names, characters, organizations, places and incidents are either the product of the author's imagination or are used fictitiously, and any resemblance to actual persons, living or dead, places, locations, events or establishments is purely coincidental.

Cover by RM Designs

ISBN: 1546519076
ISBN-13: 978-1546519072

For the Angel Babies

ACKNOWLEDGMENTS

Thank you to Renee at RM Designs for the fantastic cover for "Bittersweet." It was beyond anything I could have imagined.

Thank you to my Fabulous friends and colleagues, for all your support and encouragement. You make the journey fun.

And To Kirk, my one…my only.
None of this makes sense without you…

Chapter One

Malcolm stole his way around the old barn, dodging stray cats right and left. It was one thing to be able to blend with the local feline community, quite another to have to hang out with them.

Evading a small calico, who was too curious for her own good, Malcom managed to find his way to the orchard, to what had become his favorite apple tree. Digging his claws into the soft bark, he bolted up the trunk and into a particularly comfortable Y-branch, having somehow avoided the necessity to engage in any kitty correspondence. The moon was full, the air comfortably warm—and Malcolm was irritated as shit.

Why he ever agreed to take this job was beyond him. Sure, it seemed a perfect solution to his ongoing predicament. When his Overlord presented it to him two weeks ago, he had agreed instantly. The past couple of years had been horrible, dodging the Clowder's fumbled attempts to bring him out of his misery and back into the human world. Avoiding Kythryn.

But for Malcolm, being in his Shifter form, his feline visage, had become second nature. No, it had become first nature. For two years the mere idea of his human skin had given him hairballs. Now here he was, voluntarily shifting once a week and phoning in reports to the people who hired him. It had seemed a small price to pay to get his Clowder off his back. Still…

He had been perfectly happy sleeping in the forest, tussling with 'possums and raccoons when the mood struck him. Nothing to worry about except killing his next meal. Shifting back on a permanent basis? Malcolm knew that time had come and gone, in spite of the hope he continued to see throughout the Clowder. Doing it once a week was proving to be challenge enough, and why?

Because being human hurt too much.

Perhaps that was the source of his discontent. Sure he had this great job watching the Sweet girl, it paid well, and Kythryn was happy to continue handling his human affairs.

But that weekly shift? That's when all of the pain, all of the misery came raining down on him again, two years seeming more like two days, and it tore his fucking guts out.

The sound of the porch door banging shut pulled Malcolm from his thoughts. She was on the move again, probably off to see one of her humans, Alex or Piper. He'd stored those names in his memory, as they seemed to be the most frequent visitors.

Not the only ones, though. The place had been a veritable revolving door of people bearing gifts of food and consoling hugs. It seemed this Jessica had lost her mother recently. Malcolm got that. Losing people you loved was hard. It was nice that so many folks in the community thought enough of her to keep her fed–she was kind of skinny. Plus, she couldn't turn into a cat to escape.

She walked down the sidewalk, humming to herself, a tune Malcolm was not familiar with. He heard the jingle of keys, and the girl say, "Shit," before bending over to pick up what she had apparently dropped, then continuing on to the barnyard.

She stopped when she reached her car, an old Honda Civic that had seen better days, and she looked up at the stars. The night was clear and bright, and even with the barn light on, you could see the Milky Way and a few constellations whose names Malcolm had never bothered to learn.

She took a few shuddering breaths, and Malcolm felt her sorrow, though she was twenty yards away. He couldn't see the tears that etched her high cheekbones, or her red-rimmed eyes, but he knew they were there. He knew what loss looked like.

After a few more steadying breaths and a swipe of her hand beneath her eyes, she climbed into the car, cranked up the engine and drove off into the night.

Another boring fact to add to his report. Jessica left the house at twenty-one hundred. Returned at (yet to be determined). Yep. And for this, he exposed himself to the explosion of grief that accompanied each change.

He'd do his job, though. He'd committed to it, and was nothing if not reliable.

Although, he would probably leave off the part about her crying. No matter how much those bastards were paying him, some things were just personal.

Chapter Two

Four years ago...

Malcolm stood frozen, crouched low to the ground, the soft fur of his underbelly brushing the leaves and plants that littered the forest floor. Slowly, almost imperceptibly, he moved his front paw, taking another stealthy step toward his quarry.

The dove strutted around the base of an old oak tree, pecking the ground, looking for seeds or whatever the hell it was that doves pecked at. The point being, it was oblivious to its impending doom, as well as the mighty feline hunter who would feast on its flesh. All the hunter required was patience.

Another agonizingly slow step, and the dove was just a few feet away. Malcolm's black fur shifted in a gentle breeze, and he froze again, pacing himself, waiting. One more step and he would have his dinner. Just a few inches more, and the dove would be his.

There. Perfect. He gathered himself, powerful haunches bunched, tail angled for balance...ready...and...

BAM!

Out of nowhere, something bounded into him, knocking him off his ass and tumbling him into a thicket. He watched, stunned, as the dove he had been stalking for the last fifteen minutes went flying into the forest. Malcolm narrowed bright green eyes at the offending creature who had ruined his hunt.

Kythryn.

She had black fur that matched his almost perfectly, though she was considerably smaller than Malcolm, and sported a small white star in the center of her forehead. Kythryn was the bane of his existence.

She and her father, Seamus, had joined Malcolm's Clowder recently, and for some reason she had taken to following Malcolm around like a lost puppy dog. And no, he wasn't being ironic. Every time he turned around, there she was.

She was several years younger than Malcolm's twenty-three, and was fairly easy on the eyes in both of her forms. Plus she was obviously sporting a serious crush on him, but Malcolm couldn't manage to see her as anything more than an annoying kid. One who would not be deterred.

This stunt was just the latest on a long list of irritating shit she'd pulled. She wanted his attention, Malcolm knew that, and he tried very hard to be patient. It was never easy being the new kid in "school." But this kid was going about it the wrong way. One more episode like today and he was putting her on notice.

Giving up the hunt, Malcolm turned and headed for home. His fur was covered in burrs from that tumble into the thicket, and the only way to get rid of them would be to change. Plus, maybe Kythryn would get the message.

She didn't.

She followed him all the way back to his house, batting his tail, jumping on him. At one point he'd turned on her, pinned her to the ground with his mouth on her throat, and growled a clear warning. But the minute he let her up, she was bouncing around him again, as though nothing had happened. She was like that damned cat in the Pepé Le Pew cartoons. All she needed was a white stripe painted down her back. Or maybe she was Pepé? Hell, who could remember?

When they reached the seclusion of his back yard, Malcolm shifted and stalked to the waterproof bin he kept on the patio to grab a pair of sweats. Anticipating her shift, he pulled out an oversized sweatshirt as well.

"Hey Malcolm! I'm glad I found you! I'm so excited, I couldn't wait to tell you!" Now she sounded like that little mouse on the cartoons. The baby one that never shut up. And what was with the cartoon analogies this morning?

Malcolm threw the shirt at her without looking, but he didn't have to see her to feel her disappointment. He pulled on his sweats, waited a minute to ensure she'd put on what he had given her, then turned.

"Kythryn."

"What?" She looked so small and innocent in his shirt, her dark hair hanging in soft tangles around her face, and those big Puss-N-Boots eyes cowing up at him. Malcolm blew out a sigh, and shook his long dreadlocks out of his eyes. God, he was a pushover.

"What are you so excited about?" he asked.

"My sister is coming to live with us!"

"You have a sister?"

"Well, she's my half-sister, different mother and all, but she's really cool, and I just know you're going to love her!"

If she was anything like Kythryn, Malcolm was going to leave town.

"That's great. I'm happy for you."

"She'll be here tonight, and we're throwing a party for her. The whole Clowder is coming. You'll be there, won't you?"

Malcolm looked up at the sky, a bright blue background painted with big fluffy clouds, and searched for a way out of this. He could lie. He should lie. No, he should just flat out refuse.

But when he looked back at her she was batting those goddamned eyelashes. Sonofabitch.

"Sure," he heard himself say. "What time?"

Chapter Three

And so, several hours later, Malcolm found himself sitting on the patio nursing a beer. Unfortunately, it wasn't *his* patio. All around him cheerful Shifters chatted, their excitement level at about a ten, as they anticipated the arrival of their new Clowder member. Even the Overlord, Leonard Brandt, had made the effort to be there for the welcoming.

With her father off picking up the sister, Kythryn was playing the dutiful hostess, and was thankfully too busy to be a pest.

They had set up several tables in the yard, the majority of which were now overflowing with pot luck dishes hauled in by their guests, and Bob Parsons was manning the grill. He was a big guy with sandy brown hair and a bit more gut than was usual for a cat Shifter. However, when there was grilling to be done, he was the man for the job. Kythryn stood next to him with a platter at the ready, and he belted out a hearty laugh at something she said. Guess not everyone was as immune to her charms as Malcolm was.

He was thinking about going for another beer when a hush worked its way through the gathered crowd, all heads turning in the same direction. Malcolm repressed a sigh of relief. Finally. With the guest of honor there he could make with the pleasantries and follow them up with apologies.

Kythryn's father, Seamus Flannigan, was a tall fellow with dark blond hair and twinkling blue eyes. Malcolm had met him on several occasions during Clowder functions and found him to be a personable enough fellow, though he obviously had a blind spot where his youngest daughter was concerned.

He stood at the edge of the patio, opposite where Malcolm had secluded himself, and was being besieged by a large number of well-wishers. It wasn't often that the Clowder accepted new members. It was a process that required interviews and background checks, the whole nine yards.

But when it did happen, it was a big deal. There had been a similar gathering when Seamus and Kythryn joined the group. Once in, you were family and were treated as such, whether you liked it or not. Case in point, the huge jumble of well-meaning cats falling all over themselves to greet the new sister.

Malcolm stayed where he was, stretched his long legs out in front of him and crossed them at the ankles. He was actually born into the Clowder, so there was never a big deal like this made over him. Not that he could remember, anyway. Of course, there were always the birthday parties and such that had taken place before his parents died, but once they were gone? Well, that mostly stopped. He'd become somewhat of a loner at that point, hermit-ing himself in the house he inherited, and the Clowder mostly let him be.

The scrum of party goers was working its way into the back yard, Seamus's head peeking out above most. He was smiling, laughing, people patting him on the back in congratulations. He had a protective arm around someone, the sister, Malcolm presumed. His shouted thank yous and such could be heard above the crowd noise as he tried to free himself and his daughter from the onslaught of Shifters.

When at last they broke free from the crowd, it was like someone flipped a switch and everything went into slow motion.

The moment she emerged, tucked safely against her father's side, Malcolm's world came to a halt. She was small, like her sister, but that's where the similarities ended. Where Kythryn was thin and boyish, this girl was all curves. Her blonde hair fell in bouncing waves around her shoulders and her eyes, a perfect match to her father's, twinkled out beneath soft bangs. She was smiling politely, but her discomfort was obvious, and for reasons he couldn't fathom, Malcolm went into defensive mode.

In a blink, he found himself standing between the family and the crowd, hands raised as he shouted, "Hey, everybody, I know you're excited, but let's give the girl a chance to catch her breath!"

Laughter rang out through the Clowder and someone else hollered, "Malcolm's right! Let the girl breathe!" and the seething human tide ceased it's full court press.

Feeling things were under control, Malcolm turned to face the angel Seamus had brought into their midst.

When their eyes met, Malcolm felt the Earth shift on its axis. And when she amped up that smile and aimed it at him? Everything, the noise, the people, all of it faded into the background, and all he could see was her.

Chapter Four

"Anna!"

The spell was broken by a flurry of skinny arms and legs as Kythryn chose that moment to greet her sister with an enthusiastic embrace that took them both to the ground.

Malcolm stepped forward, prepared to jump to the rescue, but—Anna?—seemed to be taking it all in stride. After much hugging and laughter, the girls helped each other to their feet. Kythryn never stopped talking.

"And this is Malcolm."

He had been so focused on Anna, Kythryn's words weren't registering, but hearing his name brought him back to the here and now.

"Hello, Malcolm." Her voice was like music, strong and melodic, with a pleasing quality that sent unexpected shivers down his spine. She was holding her hand out to him, and he was slow on the uptake, but managed to control himself enough to shake what was offered. And when they touched? Magic.

"H-hello," Malcolm stuttered, trying to be cool, but failing miserably. He cleared his throat for a second try. "Nice to meet you. Anna, is it?"

"Yes," she said, and laughed. At him? With him? It didn't really matter. "It's so nice to meet you. And thank you."

"For what?" he asked, his brows drawn into a puzzled V.

"Crowd control." She nodded toward the scattering hoard, and Malcolm smiled.

"They can be animals," he said, and his heart did a cartwheel when she laughed at his joke.

"So." Malcolm had forgotten Kythryn was there—really, he'd forgotten everyone was there. When she spoke that single word, he glanced at her and found her scowling. That should have meant something, but his brain wasn't firing on all cylinders.

He hissed quietly when Kythryn shot him a dirty look and dragged her sister away to be introduced to the rest of the Clowder. It was all he could do to keep from trailing behind them, just to stay close to the magnificent Anna, but his eyes never left her. If she managed to become hidden by the enthusiastic throng, he shifted his position, whatever it took to keep her in his sight.

And he was pleased to see that, more often than not, she was watching him, too.

At one particular point, Kythryn leaned into her sister and whispered in her ear. Anna's beautiful eyes widened, and then her features softened as she took her sister into her arms. The next time she looked at Malcolm, the interest Anna had been showing was replaced with what looked like regret. *What had Kythryn told her?* Knowing that kid, it was hard to say, but Malcolm had a bad feeling about it.

Once Anna had been presented to everyone in attendance, and was seated at a picnic table with a plate from the potluck table, Malcolm decided he'd been patient enough.

He mustered up all the confidence he could and forced himself to make an approach.

"May I join you?" he asked. She looked up at him, and the smile she'd been sharing with her sister slipped away.

"Malcolm, hello. I-I…"

"It's okay," Kythryn said, that former scowl now replaced with a confident smile of her own. "I need to get something to drink. You guys want anything?"

Malcolm and Anna both declined, and Kythryn—thankfully—was off.

"Hi," Malcolm said as he sat, proving once again that he was a smooth operator.

"Hello," Anna repeated, and they both chuckled. When their laughter died down, they sat in silence, neither knowing what to say or how to say it.

Finally, Anna spoke, her words the absolute last thing Malcolm expected.

"Kythryn tells me you two are an item."

Malcolm aspirated the gulp of beer he'd just taken, and ultimately sprayed the rest, well, everywhere.

"She told you *what*?"

Anna frowned, dabbing at her arms where Malcolm had most inadvertently doused her.

"Please," Malcolm said, grabbing a couple of napkins from the center of the table and doing his best to help with the clean-up. "Say that again?"

Anna's eyes narrowed as she searched through the crowd for her little sister. "She said she was dating you." The words were for Malcolm, but Anna was staring death rays at Kythryn, who was smiling and waving from her spot by the coolers. "I take it you're not."

Malcolm's eyes disappeared into the back of his head as he prayed to whatever gods were out there for patience.

"No," he said. "But not for her lack of trying."

"So, she lied to me."

Malcolm sighed. "Don't be too hard on her. It's tough at her age, being new and all." He couldn't believe the words were coming out of his mouth. What he really wanted to do was pummel that little black cat to a mushy pulp.

"You're not mad at her?" Anna was watching him with a curious tilt of her head. Malcolm shrugged. "Well, I'm furious!" She threw her beer-soaked napkin onto the table and made a move to get up.

"Don't be." Malcolm placed a staying hand on her arm. Electricity shot through him again, and he could tell by her sharp intake of breath that she felt it too. "No harm done," he whispered as she reclaimed her seat and leaned into him.

"No," she whispered back, her eyes locked onto his. "No harm done at all."

Chapter Five

Malcolm spent the rest of the evening in the company of the lovely Anna. Occasionally, they were interrupted by well-meaning Clowder members offering their if-I-can-do-anythings to the newcomer, but mostly they were just in the way. Beyond that, there was nothing in Malcolm's world but her.

He learned that she was twenty-three, the same age as him, and that her mother had recently been killed in a car crash. Drunk driver crossed the median and hit her head on. She was on her way to pick Anna up from some function or another, and Malcolm felt Anna's guilt rolling off of her in waves. He assured her it wasn't her fault, but everyone knows how well that works.

What did help was that Malcolm's parents had suffered a similar fate. He knew exactly what it felt like to be all status quo one minute, and the next to have your entire world altered. He'd been close with his parents, and it was obvious Anna and her mother had been close as well.

Malcolm had never really opened up to anyone about losing his folks. They'd been gone almost two years now, but it wasn't something he cared to discuss. Until now. Now he found himself pouring his heart out to this girl he'd known for all of five minutes. But she was a girl who understood. Her condolences weren't platitudes. They were sincere and heartfelt, just as his were to her, and in this one thing, they forged a bond that would not be broken.

Somewhere in their conversation they had escaped the picnic table and found a spot beneath a crooked elm tree at the edge of the back yard. Talk turned from grief to more positive things: did they like sports (she was into basketball, where he was more of a soccer fan) and glamping vs. camping (they were both cat Shifters—duh!)

And somewhere along the line their hands had joined, and it was as natural as the rising of the moon.

When the two finally opened their eyes to the rest of the world, the stars had come out and most of the Clowder had gone home to their beds.

"Alrighty, then," Anna chuckled. "Looks like we're the last to leave the party. Is that your normal MO?"

Malcolm laughed. "No, I'm usually the guy who has one beer to be polite, then high tails it out the back door. Am I crazy Anna? Did this just happen?"

"I don't think you're crazy," she said, as she searched his eyes. "I've never been so instantly drawn to anyone before in my life."

"Neither have I."

"So what now? Do I wake up tomorrow and find out this was all a dream? This never really happened?"

"No. You'll probably wake up with me sleeping outside of your window." Anna laughed, but Malcolm was only half kidding. The idea of leaving her was twisting his stomach into giant knots.

"I don't think my father would be too keen on that." She smiled, and rubbed her thumb over the back of his hand, making him shudder.

"Probably not," he conceded. "Can I see you tomorrow?"

"Definitely."

Malcolm only just refrained from doing a touchdown dance. Instead he leaned in, pleased when she met him halfway, and touched his lips to hers for the very first time.

If he had opened his eyes, he would have seen Kythryn standing on the patio, blanket in her arms and tears streaming down her cheeks.

Chapter Six

Three Years Ago…

It didn't take Malcolm and Anna long to realize they were meant to be together, and with that amount of certainty, there was no need to wait. Within a few months they were engaged, a month more had them wed.

And the wedding was spectacular.

Anna was resplendent in white, a simple silk gown designed to flow around her slight form, nothing confining, leaving much to Malcolm's imagination.

He wore a comfortable pair of black dress slacks and a white cotton shirt, no tie.

And they were both barefoot.

They gathered with their friends and family under the light of a full moon, in a private forest on Malcolm's property. The ceremony was short, containing only the necessities, the "I dos" and the "you may kiss the bride." With the moon up and a guest list full of Shifters, there was no need to drag things out.

Once the minister pronounced them man and wife and the crowd did their cheering and catcalling, clothes came off—of the guests and wedding party alike—and the shifting began.

All around them their loved ones took their alternate forms, and within minutes the forest clearing was filled with cats of every shape and size. The Minister sat next to the happy couple, a large tailless Manx, content to chew on a paw as the rest of the Clowder settled.

Malcolm and Anna were as stunning a couple in cat form as they were as humans, his coat black as pitch, and hers snow white, with just a tiny black patch on the tip of her tail to mar her perfection.

Some of the guests were much larger than the domestic cats Malcolm and Anna turned into. There were three lions, a dozen bobcats, and a tiger who was related to Anna on her mother's side and had flown in from Jersey just for the occasion.

All in all, it was a perfect night.

And when it was over, when the prey had been caught and the guests' bellies filled, when the games had been played and the running had been done, then Malcolm led his bride to their home, to their bed.

~~~~~

Malcolm ran a hand over his forehead, wiping sweat from his brow as he shifted gears in the wheel loader he was driving. Memories of their wedding night or no, it was hot in the cab of this machine, and he reached for his water bottle to take a long drink.

He'd been working for Anderson Sand & Gravel since before he and Anna got married. Prior to that, he had been happy to live off of the inheritance his parents had left him, but now that he had a wife, he couldn't stand the idea of being idle, of not providing for her. So he'd filled out the application and they'd practically hired him on the spot. Now he drove these big machines all day long, digging up gravel and sorting it out. It was tedious and boring, but for his Anna, he would do anything.

As if his thoughts could conjure her, his phone rang and her face lit up the front of his cell. Grinning, he idled the machine down and hit accept.

"Hey, you," she said, and he could hear the smile in her voice.

"Hey, yourself," he replied. "What's up?"

"Any chance you can come home early?"

Malcolm pulled the phone away, checked the clock. It was nearly quitting time, but he had planned to have a beer with some of the guys before heading home. Anna was aware of his plans, but there was something in the way she asked that had him twitching.

"Sure," he said. "Everything alright?"

"Oh, yeah. Sure. Everything's fine. I just wanted to see you, that's all. I miss you."

Malcolm smiled wide. It hadn't taken him long to learn her tells, and that nonchalant air she was pulling had things getting tight in his workpants. He knew exactly what his kitten was saying.

"I'll be there in half an hour." Malcolm couldn't stop grinning.

"Half an hour is perfect," she said, and hung up.

Malcolm revved up the engine again and hurried to finish his work. All of a sudden there was only one place he wanted to be.

Chapter Seven

When Malcolm arrived home, he could feel something different in the air. The house was quiet, and there were no lights on at all. He walked through the living room, glanced down the hall toward the bedrooms, then entered the dining room.

The table was set with their wedding china—to his knowledge, they'd never used it before—and there were four candles burning in the center of the table, set in an X or a cross.

But that wasn't what had his breath catching in his throat.

There was his Anna, sitting in what was normally his chair, not a stitch on except a long strand of pearls Malcolm had given her for her birthday.

She was reclining in the chair with her feet on the table, legs crossed in that sexy, movie star way, and a "cat that ate the canary" grin on her face.

"What's all this?" Malcolm asked through a matching grin.

"I told you. I missed you." Anna batted those long lashes at him, and Malcolm swallowed. Hard.

"I-I…I'll be right back."

Anna sat up, planting her feet on the floor, and Malcolm caught a glimpse of her surprise as he sprinted off to the shower. No way was he touching that goddess covered as he was in gravel dust.

In record time he was showered and clean. He had to slow himself down on his way back to the dining room to keep from looking the fool. But he was naked and hungry for her, and it took every ounce of control he possessed not to sprint to her side like a sex-starved dog.

Malcolm stopped in the doorway and watched her. God she was beautiful. She sat in his chair still, her long blonde hair falling in careless waves, resting gently on the soft swell of her breasts.

But Anna seemed different now, no longer the sultry siren, bent on seducing him. She sat stick-straight and twisted the strand of pearls between her fingers, a nervous habit she'd developed. She hadn't even sensed his presence, which, for a Shifter, was a definite sign that something was off. He would play her game, though. She'd set the stage, and he wouldn't disappoint her. There would be time enough for talk—after.

Malcolm squared his shoulders and strode into the room, rounded the table and stood in front of her.

"You're in my seat," he said, the words a deep rumble in his chest. He chose to ignore it when she jumped at the sound of his voice, though she was quick to regain her composure.

"There you are," she purred, looking up at him, the shift in her attitude from a moment before confounding.

"Yes, here I am. And you're still in my seat." Malcolm smiled at her, held out his hand. She placed her delicate fingers in his palm and stood to face him. That was it. That one touch, and he was ready for her, anxious for more skin contact. All skin contact.

He pulled her against his chest, her pale skin pressing against the Swiss chocolate of his own, their bodies a tangle of dark and light, of power and grace. When their lips met it was like the first time, like every time, an explosion of passion and fire.

They landed on the floor, neither in the mood for beds or cushions. The seduction was over. There would be no more teasing, no coquettish games. This was all hunger, a driven, aching desire that had him on top of her and inside without thought or design. This was hard and physical, an act of innate perfection that would leave them both panting and spent.

They found their release together with guttural cries, and Malcolm would be sporting those scratches on his back proudly until his next change. He collapsed on top of her, trying to keep most of his weight on his forearms. She still had her arms around him, though, and when she pulled him to her, he couldn't fight it. To save her, he rolled them over so that she lay on his chest, still joined in that intimate way, their breathing stuttered as she nestled her head beneath his chin.

"I love you," she murmured, and Malcolm smiled.

"I love you, too," he said, and kissed the top of her head. "I have to say, this was way better than beers with the guys."

Anna laughed, but it was off. That thing, whatever it was that had her twisting her pearls, was back. He'd hoped for a little more of "this" time, but it seemed his Anna had things she needed to discuss. As always, she took precedence. He would do anything for her.

Gently lifting her hips, Malcolm sat them both up and repositioned her on his lap, cradling her in his arms.

"Talk to me, lover," he whispered in her ear. "Tell me what has you so out of sorts."

Anna laughed again, that strange, nervous laugh, and Malcolm pulled away from her, searched her face for a sign of something, anything.

"Nothing's wrong," she said. When he cocked an eyebrow at her she added, "Definitely not *wrong*."

"Then what is it?"

She laughed again, and the strangeness of it had Malcolm on edge. This was big. Whatever she was hiding, whatever she wasn't saying, he felt in his soul it would change his life forever.

Unable to sit any longer, he stood, offering a hand to help Anna off the floor. She took it and pulled herself up, began pacing. Malcolm watched her, all of that back and forth making his feline hackles rise under the surface of his human skin.

"Please, Anna. Talk to me."

She stopped her pacing and stood in front of him, but she couldn't or wouldn't maintain eye contact, her gaze shifting back and forth between Malcolm and the table she had so perfectly set.

He followed her gaze, truly seeing the table for the first time. Yes, he'd noticed the China and the odd candle setup, but due to his wife's magnificent pose, he'd failed to see the oblong gift box settled in the plate where he would normally dine.

"Is that for me?" he asked. She was bouncing on the balls of her feet now, wringing her hands. She nodded.

Malcolm reached for the package, turned it over, shook it. It rattled a little, but not enough for him to guess what was inside.

"Will you open it already?" Anna said in a rare moment of impatience. Malcolm raised his eyebrow again, and pulled one of the ribbon's white tails. The bow unfolded and fell away, followed by the colorful, pastel wrapping paper. The box was lidded, and Malcolm looked to Anna once more before opening it up. When she nodded, he removed the top.

The box contained an odd-looking thing, a long piece of plastic with a tiny face plate on one end. It looked like a little computer screen, only instead of computery stuff, all he saw was a couple of blue lines, in the shape of a plus-sign.

Anna was watching him, still bouncing, still wringing, obviously expecting something from him, but for the life of him, Malcolm was clueless. He held the package out to her, both hands palms up in his best "I'm sorry but I have no idea what this is" gesture, and Anna laughed. Not the anxious titters she'd been spouting all night, but a real, genuine laugh. The one that made Malcolm want to take her all over again.

"You really are oblivious aren't you?" she giggled. Malcolm shrugged, and she went to him, wrapped her arms around him and gave him one of her patented off-the-hook kisses that sealed the deal for him. When she drew away from him, she pulled his hand from her hip and placed it on her perfect, flat belly.

"Malcolm, we're having a baby."

Chapter Eight

Pregnancy was not at all what it was cracked up to be. Malcolm never knew who he was coming home to, his beautiful bride or the Bride of Frankenstein. The mood swings were horrendous, and he didn't even want to talk about the sex. One minute she was so repulsed by the idea that she ran screaming—literally screaming—from the room, accusing him of all manner of atrocities. The next thing he knew, she was all over him like a cat in heat, never mind if he'd had a long day at work and was too exhausted to think.

Malcolm supposed it was hard on her too, but he had to wonder how any species managed to survive when the females went all bonkers like this. Why would any man put himself through it more than once?

Then there were the doctor's appointments. The nurses all made over Malcolm because he was a twenty-first century father and planned to be there for Anna every step of the way. They complimented him on his dedication to the pregnancy, but his acting skills were being put to the test.

Seeing that doctor with his hands on Anna? Uhn uh. It was all he could do to keep from eviscerating the bastard. If the male's pulse had quickened even a little bit, Malcolm might have had to kill him. So far that had not been necessary.

Today's appointment, Malcolm was told, was a big one. They were going for their first ultrasound and would finally see that tiny little creature that was turning his wife into a Jekyll and Hyde.

Anna lay on a little exam table, and Malcolm sat in the visitor's chair, or whatever you call that hard plastic thing they had placed at her side. The technician was explaining the procedure, but all Malcolm heard was "eight weeks" and "heartbeat" and a whole lot of mumbo jumbo that was totally Greek to him.

Anna smiled and reached for his hand as Nancy the Technician (thank God it was a woman) announced they were about to begin. From the moment Nancy placed her magic wand to Anna's belly, a loud *woosh, woosh, woosh* assaulted Malcolm's sensitive ears.

"What the hell *is* that?" he asked.

"That," Nancy said, "is your baby's heartbeat. Only..."

Her pause didn't register to Malcolm, as he only had eyes for his beautiful Anna, and ears for that magnificent *woosh*. Anna's eyes were welling with tears, and it wasn't until he felt the wetness on his own cheek that he realized he was crying as well. What a wonderful thing this was. Why hadn't they done this ultrasound thing before? Suddenly, the horror movie of the past few weeks felt like a Snow White cartoon, with woodland creatures dancing around, bluebirds singing on his shoulder. It was the most amazing thing in the whole world.

"...and this," Nancy was saying, drawing their attention back to the computer screen, "is Baby A."

Baby A? What the hell did that mean?

"I'm sure the doctor told you that with Shifters like us, multiples are not unusual. However..." Nancy moved the magic wand again, "this is quite rare."

"What?" Malcolm asked, as Anna squeezed the shit out of his hand. "What's rare?"

"Okay," Nancy said again, squirting more gel on Anna's belly and giving that magic wand a workout. "I showed you Baby A. This," she moved toward the left, and a new blob filled the display, "is Baby B. Then here is Baby C...and yes, yes. This is Baby D!"

Four? Malcolm looked at Anna and her mouth was hanging open, probably a perfect reflection of his own expression. Four babies.

What in the hell were they going to do with *four* babies?

Aliya DalRae

Chapter Nine

2 Years Ago...

Malcolm sat in the cab of his wheel loader, pushing levers and loading gravel into a huge rock truck. Remembering that first ultrasound nearly brought fresh tears to his eyes. They'd been warned not to expect all four babies to survive. The fact that they'd heard the heartbeats at all at that early stage of pregnancy was largely due to Anna and the little ones being Shifters. So yes, that part was a gift. And a curse.

Having heard those beautiful signs of life, it made it that much harder as, one by one, the little heartbeats went silent, until there was only one tiny *woosh* left. Baby B. Just because they'd never met the little kittens didn't take away the ache that each loss left in their hearts. The Clowder tried to reassure them, reminding them that it was healthier for the pregnancy, blah, blah, blah. But Malcolm and Anna felt the sting of each loss as a permanent hole in their hearts.

Anna was terrified that Baby B would leave them as well. Even though she was nearly full term now, and the doctors reassured them that the child was healthy, Anna still lived her days in a near panic, afraid to do anything that might hurt the baby. Afraid to move. Malcolm tried to reassure her, but it was difficult when he harbored the same fears in his own heart.

Still, he clung to the doctors words, choosing to believe that all was well. It was the only way he could continue to function, to do his job and provide for Anna and Baby B. Otherwise, he would have been curled up next to his wife, waiting for the other shoe to drop.

He shook his head and reached for a lever, raising the load of gravel high, then pivoting and dumping it into the back of the truck. As he lowered the now empty bucket, his cell phone blared and vibrated against his chest where he'd taken to wearing it, just in case.

He idled down the machine and grabbed his phone. It was a text from Anna. Nine-one-one. That was their code for "Get your ass home, the baby is coming NOW!

Malcolm powered down the vehicle, and jumped from the cab, left the thing where it sat, and ran to his car.

"Is it time?" someone hollered, but he just grinned and waved. He was in the car and headed down the road in no time flat, his heart pounding against the herd of buffalo that had taken up residence in his stomach.

He pulled into his driveway, slamming on the brakes in a spray of gravel, and nearly hung himself on the seatbelt he'd forgotten to unfasten. He fumbled with the clasp, eventually freed himself, and tumbled out of the car in a scramble. Somehow he found his way into the house, and there was Anna, sitting on the couch, putting all of that Lamaze training to good use.

She smiled up at him as she panted, and Malcolm thought she had never looked more beautiful. Her golden hair was darkened with perspiration, and her cheeks were flushed as she puffed in and out. She was absolutely radiant.

"You okay?" Malcolm sat beside her and took her hand. Anna nodded and puffed some more.

"I'll get your things in the car and we can head out. Have you timed your contractions?"

Anna let out a final long breath and fell back on the couch. "Yeah," she said. "About twenty minutes apart."

"That's good, right?" Malcolm couldn't remember. Did they have lots of time? Not enough?

"We've got plenty of time," Anna said. "I've called the doctor, and he said we should come on in, though. They still consider me high risk, so he wants to keep an eye on me."

Okay. That made sense. Sort of.

Malcolm loaded Anna's overnight bag, prepacked with reading material, MP3 player loaded with all of her favorites, and a bag of snacks for him. He'd wanted to pack beer, but Anna voted against it. She said the baby was the tie breaker and was voting with Anna, so Malcolm didn't get his beer. He'd have to settle for water, beef jerky, and really bad vending machine coffee.

They made it to the hospital with time to spare. Her contractions had gone from twenty minutes apart to ten, and there was an air of anticipation in the room. The doctor was in, and said all signs were good, and the nurses were just as giddy as Malcolm and Anna were. It was like a big party, interrupted only by the horrible pains his beautiful Anna suffered with her usual grace and dignity.

After one particularly bad contraction, Anna lay gasping for breath. Malcolm held her, brushed the damp hair from her forehead and said, "So what do you suppose Baby B will be when he grows up?"

Anna smiled and said, "I suppose he'll be a doctor, don't you?"

Malcolm shrugged. "Or a lawyer. I could see our little one being skilled at debate."

"Given his father's talents in that area, I wouldn't be surprised," Anna laughed.

"Or maybe," Malcolm leaned around to look into his wife's baby blues. "Maybe he will be the first Shifter president?"

Anna bumped her head against Malcolm's shoulder. "Wouldn't that be something?" she said, but he felt her stiffen in his arms.

"Anna? Anna!"

She was shaking now, uncontrollable jerking motions pulling her away from him.

"Help!" Malcolm screamed as he held his wife to him, tried to calm her. "Help!"

Monitors were beeping all around him, and a sudden rush of nurses had him pushed to the side. The doctor ran in and went straight to Anna, looking at her eyes, then checking her all over.

The doctor yelled something, then Malcolm felt himself being pulled away from Anna. He tried to break free, to return to her side, but the people holding him were saying things like, "let them help her," and, "they need room to work." He found himself being shoved out of the room, but he watched over his shoulder as long as he could.

The last thing he saw before they pushed him down the hall was a god-awful amount of blood.

Chapter Ten

The funeral was horrible. Malcolm sat in the front of the church, staring at two shiny coffins, one of them the size of a bassinet. He knew because there was a bassinet at his house. In the baby's room.

The events following his unceremonious removal from Anna's side were a blur. He vaguely remembered the doctor coming to him in the waiting room, saying a bunch of stuff that didn't compute, and one thing that did. His wife and son were dead. He'd probably told Malcolm the hows and whys of it, but none of that registered.

All Malcolm knew was that for a brief moment he'd had a family, a beautiful, healthy, fairy tale family, and in the blink of an eye it was taken from him.

Someone sat next to him and put a hand on his arm. He looked up to see Kythryn, face blotchy from too many tears. She put her arms around him, and pulled him to her in a hug he was incapable of returning.

"I'm so sorry," she whispered, but Malcolm doubted it. Kythryn had been hateful to him and Anna from the moment it became clear that she'd lost Malcolm to her sister. Condolences from her were empty, as far as he was concerned. Then again, condolences from anyone were empty, weren't they?

For two hours he sat staring at the caskets while people filed up to him, patting him on the shoulder, offering their meaningless sympathies. Malcolm nodded when he thought he should, and

Kythryn spoke all the right words to the mourners, never leaving his side. Perhaps he should have been grateful, but her presence just reminded him of all he'd lost. Not that he needed any reminders. They were staring at him from those shiny boxes just over there.

At some point, the preacher came out and said some words, all bullshit from Malcolm's perspective. All of that, "They're in a better place," crap? No. The best place for them would have been with him, in their home, playing silly games and opening Christmas and birthday presents. That idiot had no idea what he was talking about.

After the preacher got done with his blathering, some of the Clowder members got up and spoke, again more bullshit and dribble. They'd barely known Anna, and none of them knew his son. Baby B. They had never even chosen a name for him, had decided to wait until they met him to see what name fit. Now he was dead, and she was dead, and he didn't even have a name. He was just Baby B.

Of course Kythryn spoke as well. Malcolm just tuned her right out.

And then they were loading the caskets into a hearse and loading Malcolm into a black stretch limo, along with Kythryn and Seamus. The old man was devastated, blamed himself for bringing her to the Clowder. What he was really doing was blaming Malcolm, and why not? Lord knew, Malcolm blamed *him*self.

The cars stopped, and everyone disembarked, huddled underneath a green canopy in a lovely cemetery oddly located across from a small shopping strip. But the sun was shining, there were lots of trees, and you could hear the gurgling waters of Twin Creek as it sought its way to the dam that would soon bar its path. Not a terrible place to be laid to eternal rest.

More words, more tears. Somebody sang *Amazing Grace*. Malcolm wondered at all of the church stuff—Anna had never been particularly religious—but he hadn't participated in the funeral arrangements. He'd left that to Seamus and Kythryn.

The next thing he knew, Malcolm was standing at the grave site alone. The mourners had done their thing, were probably headed back to the church to be fed after all their hard work, mourning and whatnot. He had a hazy recollection of someone trying to get him to leave, but he'd brushed them off.

He watched the cemetery workers lower the caskets into a single grave. He liked that touch, knowing that they weren't going to separate mother and child. He knew that was silly. Their souls were already out there somewhere, together, doing whatever it was that souls did when their mortal vessels died. It was Malcolm who felt abandoned.

Soon, the work was done. The coffins were covered, the canopy and chairs were removed, and the gravediggers, because that's what they were, went home to their families. They probably hugged their wives and children and thanked whatever god they believed in that it wasn't their wife. It wasn't their kid.

And Malcolm stayed.

When the sun finally slipped itself beneath the horizon and the stars peeked out one by one, when the moon stole its way into the sky, Malcolm kicked off his dress shoes. He unbuttoned his shirt and slid it from his shoulders, letting it drop to the ground. The pants were next—he'd never wear them again—and when at last he was sky clad, he called his magic forward and allowed his feline visage to take him.

On their arrival next morning, the caretakers scratched their heads at the pile of clothes that lay scattered at the foot of the fresh grave.

Malcolm was nowhere to be found.

Chapter Eleven

1 Year Ago…

Malcolm furiously paced the length of the wire pen his Clowder had so unceremoniously tossed him into. Kythryn—it was always Kythryn—poked her face near the wire, and Malcolm hissed at her. His human form would have laughed at the slack-jaw look she gave him, so to amuse himself, he hissed again. He knew this was her doing.

For a year, he had been perfectly content to wander the forests around Fallen Cross. He spent his days lying in sunbeams or resting in the crook of a nearby tree. Nights were for travelling. He ran from forest to field, on to the next forest, always on the move. When he was hungry, he hunted—birds, field mice or other rodents, he wasn't particular. Anything to fill the gnawing in his empty belly.

However, he had yet to find something to fill the chasm of his empty heart.

Last night he was on the move again, minding his own business, when some idiot dropped a net on him. He fought, hissed, scratched, bit, but they gathered him up like a bag of potatoes and brought him here. He knew they were Clowder, could smell that familiar scent. They'd carried him back in a gunny sack, dumped him in what looked like Seamus's barn. You'd think they would have been a little nicer about his abduction, but not to worry. Paybacks were a bitch.

Kythryn's startled face was replaced by the stern mien of the Clowder's Overlord.

"Calm down, Malcolm. Nobody wants to hurt you."

Malcolm's raised hackles and twitching tail told Leonard Brandt he wasn't buying it.

The older man sat on the floor next to the cage and gathered his knees to his chest, settling in for what Malcolm was sure was going to be a long lecture. He wasn't wrong.

"We just want to help you," the Overlord began. "Seamus and Kythryn have been beside themselves with worry over you. It was bad enough to lose Anna and the baby the way they did—"

Malcolm hissed again. How dare he mention them?

"—but to have you run off the way you did? You're family to them, Malcolm, and they've been sick with concern. Now, we understand the need to mourn. Don't think any of us can fault you there, but enough is enough. Kythryn has been handling your household affairs, going above and beyond to make sure you have something to come home to. But it's been over a year now. It's time to grow up, son. It's time to come home and face your responsibilities."

Malcolm growled low in his throat, and when the Overlord reached his hand toward the pen, Malcolm extended his claws and took a swipe at the proffered appendage. The Overlord withdrew his hand, and Malcolm was pleased to see the blood that dripped from the man's finger. Trap him like a rodent, throw him in a pen, and expect him to be grateful? Put your hand out there again, Leonard, and see what happens.

The Overlord sighed, and gave his head a sad toss before placing both palms on the floor.

"I didn't want to do this, Malcolm, but you're leaving me no choice. New moon's tonight. If you won't come back to us of your own accord, we're going to have to bring you back."

The Overlord pushed himself off the ground and brushed the dirt off his hands, ignoring the scratch on his finger, and the blood that still seeped from it.

"That cage is plenty big. If you're not in human form when I come back here tonight, you will be when I leave."

Malcolm watched the man's retreating back, and worked hard to ignore Kythryn's concerned questions as she followed the Overlord out the barn door.

Chapter Twelve

Malcolm paced the cage, back and forth, over and over. He'd heard there were ways to force a Shifter back into their human form, but the Overlord couldn't be serious. It was Malcolm's life, and he had absolutely nothing in the human world to live for. Why in the hell would they even bother? One thing he knew for certain, he wouldn't make it easy for them.

Kythryn returned several times, tried to talk to him, brought him food and water, but he ignored it all. He wanted nothing from that girl. Nothing. And yet she continued to pester him. When Anna was there, this bedeviling had ceased, and Malcolm hadn't given Kythryn a second thought. However, it appeared she had not given up her crazy notions nor her childish crush.

"I've kept your bills all up to date," she was saying from her seat outside the cage. "Anna had given Daddy power of attorney before the baby was...well, in case anything happened to the two of you, so he was able to sign it over to me and I've been taking care of everything. I keep it clean, your house, so it won't be all dusty when you move home, and I packed away the baby's things. I didn't think you'd want to see them right away. They're still there. I didn't get rid of anything, I just thought, well, you know..."

Malcolm rubbed a large, black paw over his eyes, then licked his pad. Every word was like fingernails on a chalkboard, and every mention of Anna and the baby was another stake to his heart.

For the first time in ages he wished for his human voice so he could tell her to shut up and go away.

"Please, Malcolm," she droned on. "Please change back. They'll be here any minute, and I don't want to see you go through that. It's horrible, I tell ya. I've read up on it and it's just awful. Please don't make them do it. Just change back now and you can pick up where you left off."

Malcolm narrowed his eyes and shifted his head, looking at her for the first time since she'd entered the barn. *Pick up where he left off? Really?*

"Hey!" she said, mistaking the eye contact and shifting herself closer to the cage. Malcolm growled, and her smile faltered as she reconsidered. "Oh. Okay."

Kythryn swung her head to the door at the same time Malcolm did, the sound of approaching footsteps announcing the Overlord's return. It sounded like half the Clowder was out there with him, and Malcolm felt the first twinge of apprehension.

The barn door slid open, and Malcolm saw the shadows of at least twenty people standing just outside. The Overlord led them in, and they moved to form a circle around Malcolm's prison, every one of them grim-faced and somber.

Malcolm moved to the center of the pen, which seemed like a wise choice, away from prying fingers, et cetera, but nobody approached him. They just stood there looking like angels of doom.

"Please, Mr. Brandt, can't you give me a little more time? He looked at me. I swear, I'm getting through to him." Kythryn was begging, but Malcolm could tell her pleas were falling on deaf ears.

When the Overlord spoke, Malcolm felt the weight of his words, and more importantly the depth of power he put behind them.

"Malcolm Gatta. We are here as your Clowder, as your family, to bring you back into the fold. Your period of mourning is over. Shift now, join us in your human form, and return to your place in the Clowder."

Malcolm turned his back to the Overlord and raised his tail high before settling back on his haunches. Yeah, it was disrespectful, but fuck him.

"Daddy, help him!" Kythryn appealed to her father when the Overlord ignored her pleas. If there was a response, Malcolm didn't hear it.

The circle of Shifters closed in on him as the Overland began to chant. Kythryn continued to beg, but her cries were soon drowned out by the chorus of voices echoing the same phrase over and over. Malcom didn't speak Latin, but he knew it when he heard it.

Ad hominem forma... Ad hominem forma...

Over and over again they repeated the words, and though he didn't understand them, he totally got their meaning.

Malcolm jumped when an electric shock zapped his back leg. He spun around with a hiss to confront whoever had attacked him, but the Clowder remained a few paces beyond the cage, eyes closed and absorbed in their chanting.

Zap! Again with the shock, only this time on his back. He flipped around, looking for something to fight, and another jolt hit him in the neck.

Malcolm yowled in frustration, biting and scratching at himself as the painful shocks continued to assault his body. He felt an odd twinge, a twisting within him, and his body contorted into an unnatural form, his legs bending, stretching, his neck and head thickening.

It was excruciating.

As a Shifter, the transformation from human to animal and back again was normally quick and painless, none of that bone cracking, skin stretching agony that the Weres had to contend with. There was something in Shifter magic that made it more natural, enjoyable even.

This, however, was not natural. Malcolm continued to yowl as his body was forced into his human shape against his will. He cried out as his clawed paws turned into human fingers before his eyes, and his fur literally fell from his skin instead of reforming as was usual.

And still they chanted. *Ad hominem forma... Ad hominem forma...*

On and on it continued, for a few minutes, an hour, a lifetime, and when his howls turned to human screams, he knew he'd been defeated.

Malcolm lay in the now-cramped cage, his human form curled into a tight ball, his breath coming in short, labored gasps. The air was cool against his bare skin, and goosebumps prickled his arms and legs, whether from the lack of fur or the magic still coursing through him, he didn't know.

The chanting had stopped, thank all that was holy, and he heard the Clowder let out a collective sigh, while someone sobbed at a distance. He made an attempt to move, to stretch, but the pain was too great, the confines of the pen too tight.

He heard, rather than saw, someone unlatching the locks that held the top of the cage in place, and then the sound of the upper section being lifted away.

Gentle hands grasped him by the arms and legs and lifted him out, then laid him on a blanket on the barn floor. Someone slid a pillow under his head.

Malcolm tested his eyes, and though it hurt, he managed to get a good look at the people who had done this to him. He wasn't ready. He still mourned his family, and he was not prepared to step back into his life.

He looked each and every Clowder member in the eyes, memorized their names. And when he glanced back at the cage and saw the aberrant pile of fur that still lay within, he knew he would never forgive them.

Chapter Thirteen

Eighteen Months Ago...

Malcolm lay in the bottom of that same damn cage he'd been confined to six months ago. This time, he'd managed to fight their spells, but he may have pushed it too far.

After that first horrific display of Clowder power, Malcolm had allowed himself to be transferred to his house. Kythryn had volunteered to watch over him until he recovered from the ordeal. It annoyed the hell out of him, but he'd been too weak to argue.

He regained his strength quickly, though, and when Kythryn's back was turned, off making him chicken soup or something equally absurd, he shifted back into his feline form.

He'd stayed human for exactly six hours.

Malcolm was several miles away before they realized he was gone. He managed to evade them for a good while, but he should have known they wouldn't give up. One moment of carelessness, and here he was, back in that damn cage, and *this close* to joining his wife and son in the hereafter.

He'd known what was coming this time, and had somehow managed to stay their magic, to hold onto his own and battle them to the bitter end. And he'd won. He was still in cat form, but *oh, the pain.*

It only took one Clowder member to lift him from the cage.

"We can't keep doing this to him," someone whispered. Malcolm thought it was Seamus.

"Well, he can't keep on the way he's been. We'll lose him forever." The Overlord.

"You're killing him!" Kythryn was crying, and he was pretty sure it was her stroking his back. God, he wished she would stop. Even his fur hurt.

"What do you suggest, then?" Seamus asked. "We do this again, there will be nothing left of him anyway. I say we just let him be. Let him mourn my Anna, and when he's ready, he'll come back to us."

The Overlord blew out a long breath, and Malcolm heard him stand and begin to pace. "Why does he have to be so goddamned stubborn?"

"Because he's a Shifter. He's still hurting, Leonard." Seamus stood and joined Brandt, disrupting the Overlord's back and forth action. "We can take him back to his house, let him know he can stay there in whatever form he chooses. Maybe if he knows we won't try to force him again, he'll stick around. At least he'd be safe here."

"Please, Mr. Brandt?" Kythryn stopped with the incessant petting to put in her tearful two cents. "I'll take care of things for as long as it takes. Just, please don't hurt him anymore."

The Overlord sighed, and even in his tortured condition, Malcolm could feel Brandt's concession.

"I don't know what else we can do? When he's recovered some, lay it out for him, Seamus. We'll just have to hope he sticks around."

Chapter Fourteen

Two Weeks Ago...

Life for Malcolm was now somewhat tolerable. After they nearly killed him, the Clowder had become obsequious, falling over themselves to earn his forgiveness. He was forever finding gifts of birds and mice on the front doorstep from feline hunting excursions, and Kythryn came by daily to make sure he had plenty of water. He prowled around the forest on his property, hunting whenever the mood struck him.

He no longer felt the need to distance himself from the Clowder, even though they never missed a chance to beg him to come back. And sometimes it was nice knowing they were there.

He would never forgive the ones who had tortured him, and they knew it. Especially the Overlord. But this was home, no matter what form he was in. He wasn't ready to resume his former life yet, the life he'd lived before Anna and Baby B had graced his world, but, well, baby steps, right?

He still couldn't bring himself to sleep in his and Anna's bed. He'd tried once, had curled himself up on Anna's pillow. It smelled of vanilla and that certain musk that was strictly hers. It was familiar and warm, but being there, wrapped in her scent, had taken him back to that horrible day, and he'd nearly run again. So the bed was off limits.

On the rare occasions he slept indoors, Malcolm chose the couch, or just stretched out on the rug. More often than not, he'd go venture into the woods and sleep under a star-filled sky. Whatever it took to get him to the next day.

He realized he couldn't keep doing that. He knew that relying on the Clowder, on Kythryn, to take care of his affairs was wrong. Aside from their poor judgment in trying to force him to change, they cared for him.

And maybe he had been a little hard on Kythryn. No, she wasn't her sister, but he was coming to appreciate all she had sacrificed to ensure there was something left if and when he decided to come home. She didn't have to do it, and he knew her reasons were her own, but still. She continued to annoy the hell out of him, but she deserved a little respect.

Malcolm was prowling around the house, looking at all of the things that had been Anna's. He remembered when she'd bought that vase, how she'd filled it with lilies and told him offhand that she liked the name Lily. He had smiled at her, wrapped his arms around her swelling belly, and told her they could name the baby anything she wanted…

The chime of the doorbell, interrupted Malcolm's musings, and he ran through the cat flap to greet his visitor. Leonard Brandt stood with his back to the door, shifting his weight from one leg to the other as he looked toward the woods, apparently deep in thought. Malcolm bumped his head against his Overlord's leg to gain his attention, then sat back on his haunches, cocking his head and twitching his ears in question.

"Hey Malcolm." The Overlord turned to him and said, "Everything okay?"

Malcolm licked a paw, then shook out his fur in response.

"So, I've got a proposition for you. A job, if you will. Are you interested?

Chapter Fifteen

Present...

Malcolm woke to the sound of a car door slamming. He'd fallen asleep in that comfortable Y-branch, but had slept in fits and turns. Too many memories haunting his dreams, too many reasons to question his decisions.

He shook the sleep from his head, stood on the wide branch and stretched, arching his back high and lifting his tail in the air, striking his favorite Halloween pose. Time to go back to work.

He jumped from the tree, landed lightly on his feet, and slid around the brooder house to the edge of the barnyard.

There she was, that chestnut hair falling around her shoulder in soft waves. She leaned over to retrieve something from the back of the car, and the little skirt she wore lifted a bit, giving Malcolm a glimpse of those long legs. She was nothing like his Anna, whose blonde hair and delicate features had given her a regal air. Still, Jessica Sweet had a way about her that made a guy sit up and take notice.

Malcolm slid into the barnyard, and stopped beneath one of the two giant maple trees that shaded the area.

He watched as Jessica pulled her head out of the car and slung her purse over her shoulder, a couple of heavy-looking plastic grocery sacks in her hand. She slammed the door and turned toward the house, but then looked over her shoulder right at Malcolm.

Changing direction, she took a couple of steps his way before stopping several feet from where he sat.

"Hey you," she cooed at him in that high pitched voice people reserved for animals and babies. "You're the new guy, aren't you?"

She knelt down, put her bags on the ground, and reached a hand out to Malcolm. "Come here baby. It's okay. Where on earth did you come from?"

There was something about this girl, something Malcolm couldn't grasp, but he found himself inching toward her. Slowly, he told himself, don't want to seem too willing.

She continued to talk to him, to coax him to her, and Malcolm decided she must be some kind of a witch, because her voice was hypnotizing, drawing him to her as though she'd cast a spell on him.

Before he knew it, he'd touched his nose to the tip of her outstretched fingers. Her scent was intoxicating, like honeysuckle and wine, and he rubbed his cheek against her hand in an attempt to take some of her sweet aroma with him. To leave some of his scent on her.

She scratched him under the chin and chuckled. "You're just a big old lover, aren't you, cat?"

Malcolm realized what he was doing and pulled away, casually, of course, like he'd meant to do it all along. Tearing his eyes from her was difficult, but one mustn't allow the humans to know they are interesting. Instead, he sat back and lifted a forepaw to his mouth, licked it and rubbed it against his cheek as though he hadn't a care in the world.

"Look at you," she laughed. "Sitting there like you're the master of your domain. I think I'll call you King, since it seems you've decided to stake your claim here. King Kat, Lord of all he sees!"

She was still smiling as she gathered up her bags and headed toward the house. "See you around, King Kat," she called over her shoulder. He could still hear her laughing as the porch door slammed shut behind her.

And that's when something happened. Something…odd. Something unforeseen. For two years, Malcolm had been filled with cold, his heart a solid block of ice. But just now? He could have sworn he felt a spark of warmth come to life deep inside him.

Malcolm sneezed, shook his head and rubbed his paw against his nose before running back to the orchard, back to that Y-Branch.

This job might not suck after all.

about the author

Aliya DalRae is the author of the Jessica Sweet Trilogy. Her debut novel, Sweet Vengeance, was published in February 2016, with the sequel, Sweet Discovery, becoming available in April 2017. The third and final book in the trilogy, Sweet Destiny, is well underway.

Learn more about Aliya, and her writing at:

Website
WWW.ALIYADALRAEAUTHOR.WIXSITE.COM/ALIYADALRAE

Like my Page on Facebook
WWW.FACEBOOK.COM/ALIYADALRAE

Follow me on Twitter
HTTPS://WWW.TWITTER.COM/ALIYADALRAE

Follow my works on Goodreads
https://www.goodreads.com/author/show/15019566.Aliya_DalRae

Once again, I thank you for reading Bittersweet, and encourage you to read and review books by Indie Authors every chance you get. Your words of encouragement or even constructive criticism help us all become better writers, and drive us to put forth our best work for you, our readers.

Follow the Aliya DalRae Amazon Author Page at
https://www.amazon.com/Aliya-DalRae/e/B01C9MZ0OW

SWEET VENGEANCE

Jessica Sweet is an orphan – Again...
At 26, the term may not truly apply, but having been abandoned by her birth parents at an early age, the death of her adoptive parents is like déjà vu all over again. Now she finds herself alone, facing a future that should be unsure; however, the visions she's been plagued with since childhood are about to descend upon her, pulling her into a supernatural world where her deepest fantasies and most harrowing nightmares will soon come true.

A monster, even by Vampire Standards...
...Raven has spent the better part of his five hundred seventy plus years fighting the evil within. His capture by an ancient breed of Sorcerers, just surfacing in the Legion's base town of Fallen Cross, Ohio, leaves him beaten and starving. Escape leads him to an old farmhouse, the single heartbeat within promising life. What he couldn't know is that the blood he now seeks will sustain him in ways he could never imagine...

Order Book 1 in the Jessica Sweet Trilogy here:
https://www.amazon.com/dp/B01C99NH3G/

SWEET DISCOVERY

Jessica Sweet...
Women are dying in Fallen Cross, people I know, people close to me.
However, it's the way they die that has me worried.
There hasn't been a murder like this in a very long time.
In fact, the last one on Legion record was about the time Raven stopped killing...

Raven...
Vampire by birth, monster by choice.
For centuries he was out of control, a murderer and so much worse.
Jessica's love broke the curse that controlled him, restoring his free will, but his savage ways remain in the past.
Or do they?
His Jessica has visions. Fate and her visions brought them together.
Now, they are threatening to tear them apart...

Order Book 2 in the Jessica Sweet Trilogy here:
https://www.amazon.com/dp/B06XYRWP8W

Made in the USA
Lexington, KY
07 November 2017